Acting Edition

I0591880

Love...or Best Offer

by Phil Olson

FOR PRODUCTION INQUIRIES

UNITED STATES AND CANADA
info@concordtheatricals.com
1-866-979-0447

UNITED KINGDOM AND EUROPE
licensing@concordtheatricals.co.uk
020-7054-7298

Each title is subject to availability from Concord Theatricals Corp., depending upon country of performance. Please be aware that *LOVE... OR BEST OFFER* may not be licensed by Concord Theatricals Corp. in your territory. Professional and amateur producers should contact the nearest Concord Theatricals Corp. office or licensing partner to verify availability.

This work is published by Samuel French, an imprint of Concord Theatricals Corp.

No one shall make any changes in this title(s) for the purpose of production. No part of this book may be reproduced, stored in a retrieval system, scanned, uploaded, or transmitted in any form, by any means, now known or yet to be invented, including mechanical, electronic, digital, photocopying, recording, videotaping, or otherwise, without the prior written permission of the publisher. No one shall share this title(s), or any part of this title(s), through any social media or file hosting websites.

For all inquiries regarding motion picture, television, online/digital and other media rights, please contact Concord Theatricals Corp.

MUSIC AND THIRD-PARTY MATERIALS USE NOTE

Licensees are solely responsible for obtaining formal written permission from copyright owners to use copyrighted music and/or other copyrighted third-party materials (e.g. artworks, logos) in the performance of this play and are strongly cautioned to do so. If no such permission is obtained by the licensee, then the licensee must use only original music and materials that the licensee owns and controls. Licensees are solely responsible and liable for clearances of all third-party copyrighted materials, including without limitation music, and shall indemnify the copyright owners of the play(s) and their licensing agent, Concord Theatricals Corp., against any costs, expenses, losses and liabilities arising from the use of such copyrighted third-party materials by licensees. For music, please contact the appropriate music licensing authority in your territory for the rights to any incidental music.

IMPORTANT BILLING AND CREDIT REQUIREMENTS

If you have obtained performance rights to this title, please refer to your licensing agreement for important billing and credit requirements.

LOVE...OR BEST OFFER was first produced at The Group Repertory Theatre, North Hollywood, California, in February 2023. The director was Doug Engalla, the assistant director was JC Gafford, the producer was Aly York, the stage manager was John Ledley, the lighting design was by Douglas Gabrielle, the sound design was by JC Gafford, the publicist was Nora Feldman, the artistic director was Doug Haverty, the marketing was by Kristin Stancato, and the graphic design was by Art & Soul Design. The cast, in order of appearance, was as follows:

CHERYL. . . . . Stephanie Colet
LORI. . . . . .Kathleen Delaney
STAN . . . . Doug Haverty
DAVE . . . . .Marc Antonio Pritchett

As the First Place Winner in the Robert J. Pickering/J.R. Colbeck Award for Playwriting Excellence, *LOVE...OR BEST OFFER* opened in March 2023 at the Tibbits Opera House, Coldwater, Michigan, produced by the Branch County Community Theatre. The director was Laurie Ludlow and the chairperson was Jennifer E. Colbeck. The cast, in order or appearance, was as follows:

CHERYL. . . . . .Amy Abrey
LORI. . . . . Nedra Kingsbury
STAN . . . . .Shaun Briscoe
DAVE . . . . Jesse Manson

LOVE...OR BEST OFFER opened in May 2023 at the Barstow Community College Performing Arts Center Black Box Theater in Barstow, California. The production company was StageCrafters Productions from Victorville, California (Producers Michael Barrett and Stephanie Brynjolfson). The directors were Stephanie Brynjolfson and Michael Barrett with lighting design by Sean Nelson. Lights and sound were operated by Paul Peterson. The publicity head was Sheila Fares. The stage manager was Kristine Nelson. The house manager was Amy Ross. The cast, in order of appearance, was as follows:

CHERYL. . . . . .Stephanie Brynjolfson
LORI. . . . . Crickett Enos
STAN . . . . Steve Millikin
DAVE . . . . Michael Barrett

CHARACTERS

CHERYL – Over fifty. Professional, businesswoman.

LORI – Over fifty. Cheryl's best friend.

STAN – Over fifty. Nerdish, computer multi-millionaire.

DAVE – Over fifty. Stan's friend and Chief Operating Officer of Stan's company.

SETTING

Cheryl's home, stage right. Stan's home, stage left.

TIME

Present Day. The play takes place over a seven-month period of time.

AUTHOR'S NOTES

Scene Breakdown

There are forty-seven, mostly short, scenes in the play that are designed to be performed continuously, without any scene or act breaks, i.e., as the lights go down on one side of the stage, they come up on the other side of the stage. With good pacing, it runs under eighty-five minutes.

If a theatre would like to add an intermission, it's up to them. One possible place for an intermission is on page 48 after Stan says to Dave, "I have no idea what I'm doing."

Production Notes

The set can be a simple black box-type set or a more elaborate, finished set.

It's up to the theatre how to show Lori and Dave when they are on the phone with Cheryl and Stan. For the sake of the script, we will say, "enters on platform," when Lori and Dave are on the phone. Otherwise, they will enter directly into Cheryl and Stan's homes.

Some theatres may elect to have all actors remain on stage at all times, instead of entrances and exits, and use lighting to show which actors are "on."

Options to show Dave and Lori include them entering on two platforms, stage left and stage right, or on a single platform upstage center.

Another way to show them is by appearing behind a scrim where lighting reveals the characters.

Another option, have TV screens on the wall showing the actors, live, while face-timing on their cell phones, or project them on a screen.

Options for using cells phones include using Bluetooth earpieces, FaceTime, or the speaker on the phone.

ACKNOWLEDGEMENTS

Like many of my plays, my goal with *Love...or Best Offer* was to write a comedy with some very personal, heartfelt emotional moments.

Love...or Best Offer was inspired by the real love of my life, Nancy, whom I met online. Nancy has qualities similar to the character, Cheryl, in the play; she's a licensed fiduciary, she has a special needs daughter, and a son, as in the play. Thank you to Nancy for giving me the "okay" to write about her, including some emotional challenges that she has faced, and for all the laughs that we've had. Thankfully, the real life story has a happy ending, as does the play.

Love...or Best Offer had twenty-five readings throughout the country that helped in the development of the play. A big thanks to the theatres that put on the readings, including: The Group Repertory Theatre, North Hollywood, CA, The Mighty Richland Players, Orangeville, IL, Lake of the Woods Players, Locust Grove VA, High Desert Center for the Arts, Victorville, CA, Pequot Lakes Theater, Pequot Lakes, MN, Persimmon Tree Players, Fluvanna County, VA, Broadway Vista Theatre, Vista, CA, Canyon Theatre Guild, Newhall, CA, Grand Island Little Theatre, Grand Island, NE, Showcase Players, Colby, WI, Stage Coach Theatre, Boise, ID, Friends of the Arts, Renville, MN, Stage 212, LaSalle, IL, Brunswick Little Theatre, Southport, NC, History Boy Theatre, Jefferson, IA, Mama Moon Theatre, Volga City, IA, Redlands Footlighters, Redlands, CA, Catskill Community Theatre, Oneonta, NY, and the Fort Worth Community Arts Center, Fort Worth, TX.

And finally, a giant thank you to my friends at Concord Theatricals/ Samuel French for publishing *Love...or Best Offer*.

– *Phil Olson*

(Stage right is CHERYL's home office, stage left is STAN's home office. A small table, downstage right, on Cheryl's side, has a laptop computer on it. A small table, down stage left, on Stan's side, has a laptop and two small Lord of the Rings figurines. There are two door openings, one upstage left, another upstage right. There are two other openings, center stage left and center stage right that open to a platform for LORI and DAVE.)*

(Lights up stage right. CHERYL enters while talking to someone behind her. We don't see him.)

CHERYL. *(Rapid fire.)* Thanks so much for a wonderful time, I'd invite you in but my place is a total mess, and I have a real busy day tomorrow, lots of work tonight, and I feel like I'm coming down with something, must be going around. Anyway, thanks so much, take care, buh bye.

(She closes the door, hits speed dial on her cell phone.)

I am gonna kill her.

LORI. *(Enters on platform on her cell phone.)* Hey, Cheryl. How did it go?

CHERYL. No more blind dates.

LORI. It couldn't have been *that* bad.

CHERYL. He brought his kids.

---

* A license to produce *Love...or Best Offer* does not include a license to publicly display any branded logos or trademarked images. Licensees must acquire rights for any logos and/or images or create their own.

LORI. Why didn't he get a babysitter?

CHERYL. His kids are adults.

LORI. That's sweet. He's spending quality time with 'em.

CHERYL. He asked me to split the check.

LORI. I've had worse.

CHERYL. We went to Hooters.

LORI. Nope. You win.

CHERYL. And you thought he would be a good match?

LORI. Think of it as a practice run. You've been out of the market since the Ice Age. You need it.

CHERYL. No, I don't.

LORI. Listen to me, Cheryl, as your therapist –

CHERYL. You're not my therapist.

LORI. As your best friend, you need to start dating. I'm worried about you.

CHERYL. I'm fine. And it's been twenty-nine years since my last date. It's not that I'm rusty, I'm corroded.

LORI. You need practice. I have another guy for you. He does my taxes.

CHERYL. I'm not doing this again.

LORI. Okay, no more blind dates. We'll go to online dating.

CHERYL. Oh, no. That's for young people.

LORI. Well, you're young at heart.

CHERYL. The other day I pulled a hamstring putting on my shoe.

LORI. That's nothing. Last night I sprained my back, *sneezing*.

CHERYL. See?

LORI. I know. One minute you're young and fun, and the next minute you're turning down your car stereo so you can *see* better.

CHERYL. Young people have what I don't have, hope.

LORI. It's not just a young thing. Online dating is a party that everyone is at.

CHERYL. Is it a fun party?

LORI. No, it's a nightmare.

CHERYL. *(Sarcastic.)* Oh, well, you convinced me.

LORI. Everyone does it. It's like online shopping.

CHERYL. I'd rather stick with Amazon. They never reject me.

LORI. You have to do it. Now, promise me you'll at least try.

CHERYL. Lori, I don't need a man in my life.

LORI. Cheryl, I beg to differ.

> *(Lights down, stage right.* **CHERYL** *and* **LORI** *exit.)*

(Lights up, stage left. **STAN** *enters on his cell phone.)*

STAN. Hey, Trish, it's Stan... No, nothing's wrong, I just called to say hi... I know I just saw you ten minutes ago. I just miss you already...you're right, boundaries, got it, but, before you go, I just want to say... Okay I know we just met *tonight*, but I was wondering if you'd like to go on a *cruise* with me...too soon?... Yeah, you're right. How about dinner tomorrow?... You're moving? Where?... Undisclosed... Oh, you're in the C.I.A.? I thought you were an accountant... Okay, how about breakfast?... You're leaving in an hour?... Well, can I visit you? – Hello? Hello?... Hmm, must be a bad connection.

(Lights down, stage left. **STAN** *exits. Lights up, stage right.* **CHERYL** *enters, on her cell phone as* **LORI** *enters on the platform on her phone.)*

LORI. You need to get out there. You've been despondent for two years.

CHERYL. I'm happy with my despondence.

LORI. What would Steve want?

CHERYL. Oh, don't do that.

LORI. You've successfully completed the mourning period. Steve would want you to be happy.

CHERYL. I'm not ready for happiness.

LORI. You have a lot of anxiety and it's not healthy. You're not in a good place right now.

CHERYL. "Not all those who wander are lost."

LORI. What is that, Socrates?

CHERYL. No, Gandalf.

LORI. Whatever. You need to find a guy to help carry your angst. Think of him like an emotional pack mule.

CHERYL. It's late. I gotta go.

LORI. Love you, Cheryl.

CHERYL. Yeah, yeah.

> *(Lights down stage right.* **CHERYL** *and* **LORI** *exit.)*

(An hour later. Lights up stage left. **STAN** *enters, followed by* **DAVE**.*)*

STAN. So, what's up, Dave? A little late for you, isn't it?

DAVE. I was just wondering how the date went.

STAN. I thought it went well.

DAVE. Uh huh.

STAN. Turns out Trish is in the C.I.A. She's moving, so not really sure what the future is.

DAVE. Yeah, about that. I just got off the phone with her.

STAN. Trish? How is she? Hey, thanks for setting me up, by the way.

DAVE. Did you tell her you have a *Lord of the Rings* figurine collection?

STAN. *(Holding up figurines.*)* I do. And it's awesome.

DAVE. And that you put on little plays with 'em?

STAN. Because they're on a quest. Duh.

DAVE. Yeah. You might wanna hold off on sharing that kind of information.

STAN. Until when?

DAVE. I'd wait until, ahh...never... Never tell 'em. Not even if you get married.

STAN. *(Laughs.)* You're funny.

DAVE. Look, I'm sorry, but Trish doesn't want you to call her.

STAN. Why? What did I do?

DAVE. Oh, there just isn't enough time.

---

*A license to produce *Love...or Best Offer* does not include a license to publicly display any branded logos or trademarked images. Licensees must acquire rights for any logos and/or images or create their own.

STAN. Well, do you have anyone else you can set me up with?

DAVE. Well, Trish was the third one, and, ahh, no, there's no one else.

STAN. Okay. That's it, then. I'm gonna join a monastery.

DAVE. Monasteries don't have wifi.

STAN. I will *not* join a monastery.

DAVE. You need to try online dating.

STAN. Oh, no, I'm not doing that.

DAVE. Everyone does it. I met my girlfriend online. I'm surprised we're still together. She returns everything she gets online.

STAN. I tried it. It doesn't work.

DAVE. What did you try?

STAN. Bumble.

DAVE. Is that the one where the woman has to make the first move?

STAN. Yeah. No one ever swiped right on me. The algorithm is flawed.

DAVE. Yeah, that's probably it. How about Tinder?

STAN. Tinder is a confidence killer. You have to be smoking hot and have six-pack abs, and go parasailing while you're cliff diving.

DAVE. How about eHarmony?

STAN. I tried 'em all, Blender, Hinge, *Ancestry.com*... Not a single smiley face. They don't work.

(Looking at his computer.)

Wait, I haven't tried, WomenBehindBars.com.

DAVE. Try it. She'll steal your heart, then your wallet. Listen, women don't like desperate guys.

STAN. I *am* desperate. To find love. Or best offer.

DAVE. You tried that. Your ex-wife wasn't on the same page.

STAN. Jill just didn't give me a chance.

DAVE. Jill is eighteen years younger. She married you for your money.

STAN. She was mature for her age.

DAVE. "Mature?" Her favorite drink is "juice box."

STAN. No, it isn't. It's Sunny D. Look, I'm not giving up on love, and I'm not gonna beat myself up about the divorce. Half the people in the country get divorced.

DAVE. Do half end up with the husband losing thirty million dollars to a witch that ran off with the pool boy?

STAN. I don't get it. I thought she loved me.

DAVE. She did. Thirty million dollars worth. Good thing you have a prenup.

STAN. I don't understand women.

DAVE. Quick tutorial. They grew up watching *Cinderella*. Too many of 'em want a big-dollar Prince Charming to sweep 'em off their feet. They want guys that are confident, but not cocky. Handsome, tall guys that have cool cars and big houses. And if you can make her laugh, bingo. So, here's the deal, you need to find one that doesn't want all your stuff.

STAN. And where do I find that?

DAVE. Have you tried, "Friends, Love, or Whatever?" It's new.

STAN. I don't think so.

DAVE. You start off on a Zoom date. No pressure. It's where I met my girlfriend.

STAN. I'm done with online dating.

DAVE. What do you have to lose?

STAN. Thirty million dollars.

DAVE. You can't give up. Now, look, as your friend, and Chief Operating Officer, you're kind of falling apart and your company is starting to suffer because of it. Now, get out there and find love. Or best offer.

STAN. I'll think about it.

DAVE. And promise me you won't be desperate.

STAN. Too late.

DAVE. I'll put together your profile.

(He exits.)

STAN. *(Follows* **DAVE** *out.)* Bye, Dave.

(Lights down, stage left.)

(The next day.)

(Lights up, stage right. **CHERYL** *enters with* **LORI**.*)*

LORI. *(Looking at her cell phone.)* You need to pick a dating site. How about Match.com?

CHERYL. I'm having second thoughts.

LORI. What's the worst thing that can happen?

CHERYL. I can get murdered.

LORI. I think you're a little paranoid.

CHERYL. Oh, yeah? "Hey, let's go for a hike." They all wanna go for hikes. What's the deal with hiking? They get you out in the middle of nowhere, no cell service. Push you off a cliff. Dead. Broken neck. Headline the next day, "Dead woman found near hiking trail. Looks like another bad online date."

LORI. *(Ignoring her, looking at her phone.)* How about Tinder?

CHERYL. No! That's just for hooking up. What about "OkCupid?"

LORI. No, that one's free. It's known as "badcredit.com." You need someone with money, who can afford a dating website.

CHERYL. So, which one?

LORI. Well, what's your goal?

CHERYL. My goal last year was to lose ten pounds. I only have fourteen to go.

LORI. I saw a recent study showing that women who carry a little extra weight live longer than the men who *mention* it.

CHERYL. That sounds right.

LORI. *(Looking at her phone.)* What's your goal for dating? Some sites are pretty specific. There's "Furry Mate," for those who like to dress up like animals.

CHERYL. Is that even real?

LORI. "Farmers Only?"

CHERYL. For those who'd like to plow your south forty?

LORI. Plenty of Fish?

CHERYL. Okay, now you're just floundering.

(Laughs to herself, **LORI** *doesn't respond.)*

That was a joke.

LORI. I beg to differ... How about, "Our Time?" It's for people over fifty.

CHERYL. This isn't our time. Our time was thirty years ago.

LORI. What do you want out of this?

CHERYL. I don't want anything. You're the one that came up with it.

LORI. I'll tell you what you *need*. You need to be happy and enjoy life again. Here's one called, "Friends, Love, or Whatever." You meet on Zoom before going out. There's no pressure. If it's going bad, end the meeting. Blame it on the internet.

CHERYL. Remember the good old days when you just put on makeup and went outside. "Here I am!"

LORI. I prefer the old fashioned way of meeting people through alcohol and poor judgement... But we live in the present, and that requires a profile.

CHERYL. I don't wanna be dishonest with some poor guy looking for companionship.

LORI. You *won't* be. That's why *I'm* writing your profile. What are you looking for?

CHERYL. *(Deep breath.)* For a man who likes to travel, but has no baggage.

LORI. *(Writing on cell phone.)* Travels without baggage. So, *homeless*. What else?

CHERYL. Looking for a guy with no ego.

LORI. That narrows the field to...no one.

CHERYL. No weirdos, no mamma's boys, no mennonites.

LORI. How about, "controlling woman looking for a man of few words."

CHERYL. Perfect.

LORI. I'll put in, "must be over six feet tall, have a six figure income, and six-pack abs."

CHERYL. That's a Chippendale dancer.

LORI. Exactly... You need a rich stud, someone who will take you places and spend huge amounts of money on you.

CHERYL. I have my own money. I don't need a rich guy to pay for me.

LORI. The guy always pays. It's called chivalry. It's in the Bible.

CHERYL. Where in the Bible?

LORI. The Book of...

　　　(Thinks.)

Mormon.

CHERYL. I don't want a guy that thinks he can buy me.

LORI. Why? Let him think it.

CHERYL. I want a guy with character and integrity.

LORI. *(Laughs, then stops.)* Oh, you're serious.

CHERYL. I mean, he has to be able to support himself. And be squared away. And not a serial killer.

LORI. Okay, what are your good qualities?

CHERYL. I'm fluent in sarcasm.

LORI. That is *so* cool.

CHERYL. Really?

LORI. No! That was sarcasm!... I'll put, "Likes long walks on the beach."

CHERYL. That's hiking with melanoma.

LORI. "Likes to laugh."

CHERYL. Who doesn't like to laugh? Might as well just put, "likes to breathe, likes to eat, sometimes bathes."

LORI. I'll figure it out. You need a good photo. Show me something inviting.

> (**LORI** *holds up her phone to take a photo.* **CHERYL** *purses her duck lips and sticks out her butt.*)

Really?!... Show some shoulder.

> (**CHERYL** *tries.*)

Nope. Be sexy.

> (**CHERYL** *tries.*)

Nope. Try laughing.

> (**CHERYL** *tries.*)

Good Lord. I have some photos from our Napa trip. I'll use those.

> (*Looks at her watch.*)

Oh, shoot, we gotta go.

CHERYL. I'm not on board with this.

(She exits.)

LORI. *(Follows her out.)* You will be.

>   *(Lights down, stage right. Lights up, stage left.*
>   **STAN** *enters, on his phone, talking to* **DAVE**.*)*

DAVE. *(Entering on platform.)* Okay, let's go over your profile. Everyone likes the "i-n-g's," hiking, biking, climbing.

STAN. I prefer eating, drinking, and sleeping.

DAVE. You gotta go with something interesting like, "enjoys CrossFit," whatever that is.

STAN. "CrossFit?" I feel good getting my leg through my underwear without losing my balance.

DAVE. You need something alluring.

STAN. How about, "Beefcake looking for food processor."

DAVE. What does that even mean?

STAN. "Stud muffin awaiting his turkey baster"... "Mr. Goodbar looking for Godiva."

DAVE. Please stop... I'll come up with something. Do you have a photo?

STAN. Not current.

DAVE. Take one that says, "Hey, are you up for this?"

STAN. Okay, just a second.

>   *(**STAN** takes a horrible selfie.)*

DAVE. Perfect. How are your flirting skills?

STAN. I don't know.

DAVE. Women love a guy who can flirt. Let's see you try. Give me your best flirt.

STAN. *(Worst, cheesy flirt ever.)* Hey, there, is your name "Wifi?" 'Cause I am feelin' a connection.

DAVE. Never do that again.

STAN. Actually, I think I nailed it.

DAVE. No, you did not.

(Lights down, stage left. **STAN** *and* **DAVE** *exit.)*

(A few days later.)

(Lights up, stage right. **CHERYL** *enters, on her phone talking to* **LORI**.*)*

CHERYL. I have some hits.

LORI. *(Enters on platform on her phone.)* Let me see 'em. Do a screen-share.

> **(CHERYL** *sits at her desk, screen-shares with* **LORI**.*)*

Nope...nope...nope...nope. Wait, who's the hottie?

CHERYL. Jerry. He's online.

LORI. Send him a happy face. No, wait, do a fist bump, it's more casual.

CHERYL. He asked me to dinner.

LORI. No dinner. Zoom meeting only.

CHERYL. He wants to take me to Morton's Steak House.

LORI. Go to dinner!

CHERYL. I don't know.

LORI. Have you had their fillet? Get the big one. Bring some home for me. And meet him there. Park a block away so he doesn't see your car, just in case he's a murderer.

CHERYL. I hate this.

LORI. It gets better.

CHERYL. No, it doesn't.

> *(Lights out, stage right.* **CHERYL** *and* **LORI** *exit.)*

(A few days later.)

(Lights up, stage left. **STAN** *enters, on his phone.)*

STAN. I've got no replies. Nothing.

DAVE. *(Enters on platform on his cell phone.)* Don't worry about it. Rejection builds character.

STAN. Then I have the best character ever.

DAVE. Your age and distance requirements are probably too narrow. What are they?

STAN. Anyone between thirty and ninety years old that lives within three hundred miles.

DAVE. Let's expand that to all fifty states.

STAN. You know what I think it is, I'm overqualified.

DAVE. Sure, you are. *Or...*you're aiming too high. You need to set the bar lower.

STAN. It can't go any lower. Maybe I should change my profile. Should I mention my business?

DAVE. No. Do not talk about your business. Tell 'em you're a computer programmer, which is true. And don't talk about your houses, your cars, your boats or your helicopter. The wrong women will glom on to that, and you'll end up where you were before. Unless you're just looking for a hookup, in which case, yeah, mention your money.

STAN. So cynical.

DAVE. You need to appeal to them on your character. That's the only way you'll find true love.

STAN. I'm gonna find her.

DAVE. Optimism. I like that. Okay, back to your profile. I'll put down that you like to hike.

STAN. I don't like to hike.

DAVE. But women do for some reason. They all love to hike.

STAN. Shouldn't I just be myself?

DAVE. Oh, no! Absolutely not! I mean, you should try to be honest, and whatnot, but you also want someone to like you, and honesty doesn't always mesh with that goal. In other words, don't be honest.

STAN. I hate this.

DAVE. Never give up! Never surrender!

(Lights down, stage left. **STAN** *and* **DAVE** *exit.)*

(Five weeks later.)

(Lights up, stage right. **CHERYL** *enters, then* **LORI***.)*

LORI. So, how did your date go last night?

CHERYL. During dinner, he told me he loved me.

LORI. Ew.

CHERYL. Then he *cried*.

LORI. Okay, not ideal.

CHERYL. Big loud tears.

LORI. Yikes...when are you gonna see him again?

CHERYL. Never!

LORI. Don't give up on him.

CHERYL. Then he asked for a picture. Of my *feet*.

LORI. Moving on. So where are we? You have any good prospects? I mean you've gone out with enough. There must be *someone* that toots your horn.

CHERYL. I don't even think my horn works.

LORI. We're gonna fix that.

CHERYL. They never look like their photo.

LORI. Well, have enough drinks until they do.

CHERYL. I'd be drunk before appetizers.

LORI. What happened with Michael?

CHERYL. He took me to a funeral.

LORI. Wow. Okay. Carl?

CHERYL. He just got out of prison.

LORI. Well, he *did* say he lived in a gated community... Harold?

CHERYL. He talked about himself the whole time. End of the night he didn't know my name.

LORI. Well, Cheryl is a tough name for men. I mean, it does have two *syllables*... What about Nathan?

CHERYL. That was going pretty well until his wife called.

LORI. His wife?!

CHERYL. With a reminder to pick up a carton of eggs.

LORI. That's horrible! Married men should have their *own* dating website.

CHERYL. *That's* your takeaway?

LORI. No, it's disgusting... When are you gonna see him again?

CHERYL. Never! I think I'm just resigned to being a happy cat lady.

LORI. You're allergic to cats.

CHERYL. Details.

LORI. Don't give up.

CHERYL. What about you? Have you found anyone online?

LORI. Last week I went out with a sixty-year-old virgin whose photo was from his high school yearbook.

CHERYL. Where did you go?

LORI. Del Taco.

CHERYL. "Del Taco?"

LORI. He had a coupon. Which expired. But he had a second one that worked.

CHERYL. Sounds like a catch.

LORI. While he was eating his crispy chicken tenders, he leans over and says, "Hey baby, your place or mine?"

CHERYL. Ugh.

LORI. I said, "Both. You go to your place, I'll go to mine."

CHERYL. I never thought dating would be so hard. And it's hours of my life that I'll never get back.

LORI. You need to relax. Take life with a grain of salt. And a slice of lemon. And a shot of tequila.

CHERYL. I don't know if I can do this.

LORI. Yes, you can. Just remember, nobody tells the truth on their profile. They're all ten years older and twenty pounds heavier than their pictures. That's why you should start with Zoom dating. What happened to Zoom dating?

CHERYL. They talked me into in-person dinner. I was weak. Never again.

LORI. Don't you have a dinner date this Friday?

CHERYL. Gary, the doctor. I'm not gonna go.

LORI. Don't cancel.

CHERYL. But you just said...

LORI. Roll the dice on the doctor. How long has it been, since you...

(Making bed squeaking noises.)

Eee ee eee ee eee ee.

CHERYL. A long time.

LORI. Listen to me, Cheryl, all men want is to get into your grundies.

CHERYL. "Grundies?"

LORI. Granny undies. And you need to let him know you're open for business. Set a thirst trap and wait for the bait. Write this down, "Did you have Campbell Soup this mornin'? Cause you're lookin' mmm mmm good."

CHERYL. That's frightening. I'm not going. I'm done.

LORI. You have to kiss a lot of frogs.

CHERYL. I've kissed the whole frog farm. None of these guys stack up to Steve.

LORI. Is that what you want? Another Steve?

CHERYL. I wanna heal my broken heart.

LORI. No one is going to compete with Steve. Get that out of your head.

CHERYL. I've been doing this for five weeks. I'm exhausted.

(She exits.)

LORI. *(Following her out.)* There is no rest for the weary.

(Lights out, stage right.)

(A few days later.)

(Lights up, stage left. **STAN** *enters, followed by* **DAVE**.*)*

DAVE. Any good news?

STAN. I had two dates.

DAVE. Are you serious?

STAN. Serious as a heart attack. Thank you, Lipitor.

DAVE. What happened?

STAN. Well, the first one was eighty-nine years old. She had a walker and an oxygen tank. She thought I was her Uber driver. She was a good tipper but not really my type.

DAVE. What about the second one?

STAN. I convinced that one to meet me at Starbucks.

DAVE. So, what happened?

STAN. We talked. For an hour. She's a programmer, too. I told her a joke.

DAVE. Oh, no.

STAN. How many programmers does it take to change a lightbulb?

DAVE. I give up.

STAN. None. It's a hardware problem.

(He laughs.)

DAVE. So...how long did the date last after *that* joke?

STAN. Oh, gosh, another five minutes.

DAVE. Are you going out with her again?

STAN. I'd like to but she's moving to Costa Rica.

DAVE. Listen, don't give up. Getting a first date is a giant step, and you achieved that. So, yay. Let's try to get a second date now. Do you have any prospects?

STAN. I'll take a look.

>*(**STAN** goes back to his computer. **DAVE** looks over his shoulder.)*

>*(Lights up, stage right. **CHERYL** enters, followed by **LORI**. **CHERYL** goes to her computer.)*

LORI. *(Looking at her phone.)* What about this one? Stan...

CHERYL. *(Looking at her computer.)* Stan Jensen?

LORI. *(Looking over **CHERYL**'s shoulder.)* "Searching for the ring of power in Middle-earth."

CHERYL. That's a *Lord of the Rings* reference.

STAN. Here's one. "Looking for accomplished man who's more fun than a two hundred foot waterslide."

DAVE. Next.

LORI. "I'm a fun-loving guy who has absolutely no interest in committing murder."

CHERYL. That's a joke, right?

STAN. "Looking for a man who is tall, dark and *has some*."

DAVE. NO!

LORI. He looks promising. "Never been in jail except when playing Monopoly." And...send.

>*(She hits return.)*

CHERYL. What did you do?

STAN. *(Looking at his computer.)* Whoa! A Zoom invite... Cheryl...Okay, okay, don't panic, do not panic.

>*(Hits a key.)*

LORI. Give him a try.

CHERYL. No, no, I'm not going to –

STAN. Is this Cheryl?

CHERYL. What's happening?!

STAN. Cheryl? It's Stan. You invited me to a Zoom meeting.

CHERYL. Oh, crap. Can you hold for a minute?

STAN. Sure.

> (**CHERYL** *gets up, glares at* **LORI**, *adjusts herself.* **STAN** *looks at* **DAVE**.)

A little privacy?

DAVE. Yeah, sure, I'll just...be in the game room.

> (**DAVE** *exits.* **CHERYL** *fixes her hair.*)

LORI. Your hair is perfect.

> (*Looks at her nose.*)

How do you get it to come out of your nose like that?

CHERYL. *(Cries.)* Oh!

LORI. I'm joking. You look great.

STAN. You okay?

CHERYL. Yeah, just...doing stuff.

LORI. *(To Cheryl's computer.)* Hi, Stan, I'll let you two talk. See you, Cheryl.

> (**LORI** *exits giving* **CHERYL** *the "call me" signal.*)

STAN. I'm not interrupting, am I?

CHERYL. *(Sitting back down.)* No, that was just a friend. She's gone, hopefully. Hi.

STAN. Hi, how are you?

CHERYL. I'm good. You?

STAN. I'm great. Thanks for the Zoom invite.

CHERYL. Oh, well, it just happened... So, here we are.

STAN. Have you been on a lot of dates? Am I allowed to ask that? You don't have to answer.

CHERYL. A few.

STAN. I'm divorced. Dave calls my ex-wife, "The Witch." I probably shouldn't have said that.

CHERYL. Who's Dave?

STAN. Just a friend. He gives me bad dating advice.

DAVE. *(Offstage.)* I do *not!*

CHERYL. We should set him up with my friend, Lori. They might get along.

STAN. Sure, okay. So...checking off the list, here; previously married?

CHERYL. Widow.

STAN. Oh, my gosh, that is very sad. I am so sorry.

CHERYL. Thanks. That's sweet of you.

STAN. *(Surprised, flattered.)* It is? Oh, okay...Umm, so how are you doing? It must be tough. How long ago did he?...

CHERYL. I'm fine. Really. Maybe we should talk about something else.

STAN. Yeah, yeah, right, okay, so...what kind of things do you like to do?

CHERYL. Well...I like to read books.

STAN. Really? So do I. Do you have any favorites?

CHERYL. Oh, umm...*Lord of the Rings.*

STAN. *Lord of the –*

> (**STAN** *gets emotional, gets up, away from the computer, does a fist pump, mouths, "Yes!".*)

CHERYL. You okay?

STAN. *(Goes back to the computer, calmly.)* Yeah, I just... dropped something. So, *Lord of the Rings.* Yeah, that's a decent trilogy.

CHERYL. Are you a fan? I saw the "Middle-earth" reference in your profile.

STAN. "Fan?" Not sure that's the word you would use, but, yeah.

CHERYL. "We shall ride wargs to the mountain of fire for a romantic evening at the cracks of doom."

STAN. *(Orgasmic.)* Ohh!

> (**STAN** *puts up his index finger to* **CHERYL** *a la "give me one minute," he gets up, walks away from the computer, in ecstasy.*)

CHERYL. You okay?

STAN. Yeah, I'm good.

> *(To himself.)*

Pull it together.

CHERYL. We can do this later.

STAN. No, no, I'm okay.

> *(Calmly goes to computer.)*

So, what is it that you do?

CHERYL. I'm a licensed fiduciary.

STAN. Oh, great... I don't know what that is.

CHERYL. I manage special needs trusts.

STAN. Oh, well, good for you. That seems like a very noble profession.

CHERYL. How about you? What do *you* do?

STAN. I'm a...computer programmer.

CHERYL. Oh, okay. Do you like it?

STAN. Oh, it's kind of boring. Yeah, I don't know why I said that. It's not boring at all, not for me. All those ones and zeros. It can get crazy. Do you like coffee?

CHERYL. I live on it.

STAN. Me, too. Definition of a programmer: A machine that turns coffee into *code*.

　　　(He laughs, no response from **CHERYL***.)*

Because you use computer code to program –

CHERYL. Yup.

　　　(Looks at her phone.)

Oh, shoot, I'm getting a call. It's one of my clients. I'll call him back.

STAN. Would you like to have coffee sometime? I mean, we can meet in a well-lit, busy location in case you're worried that I'm a serial killer.

　　　(He laughs, cuts it short.)

Oh, why did I say that? Sorry, I'm really nervous.

CHERYL. Why?

STAN. Oh, gosh, I don't know. You seem more squared away than most. I mean, you seem normal and have a good job, and you like *Lord of the Rings*. And you never hear the word, "normal" and "*Lord of the Rings*" in the same sentence.

CHERYL. I guess I'm old school.

STAN. So...coffee?

CHERYL. How about Zoom coffee?

STAN. Sure. Zoom coffee.

CHERYL. Saturday at nine?

STAN. Great. See you then.

>   *(He hits a key.)*

Yes! Yes!

CHERYL. I'm still here.

STAN. Sorry.

>   *(Flips his computer down.)*

Idiot!

>   *(Lights down, stage right. **CHERYL** exits. **DAVE** enters, stage left.)*

"We shall ride wargs to the mountain of fire –"

>   *(Orgasmic.)*

Ohh ohh.

DAVE. *(Re: **STAN**'s writhing in ecstasy.)* Are you okay?

STAN. She's the one.

DAVE. The one what?

STAN. The one I'm going to marry.

DAVE. And you know that after one Zoom call?

STAN. She quoted *Lord of the Rings*.

DAVE. I told you not to mention that.

STAN. No, no, it was a good thing. She's into it.

DAVE. How is that possible?

STAN. I'd like you to be my best man.

DAVE. Can you hear yourself? You sound insane.

STAN. You're the one that told me to do online dating. I owe it all to you.

DAVE. Stop it. It was just a Zoom call. Do not jump into anything.

STAN. She has a friend you might like, Lori. Hey, she can be the maid of honor.

DAVE. Listen to me, take this one slow.

STAN. Okay, will do... It'll be a spring wedding.

DAVE. Stop it!

> *(Lights down, stage left.* **STAN** *and* **DAVE** *exit.)*

(The following Saturday.)

*(Lights up, stage right. **CHERYL** enters holding coffee, followed by **LORI**.)*

CHERYL. I don't know. I'm not sure if there's any chemistry there.

LORI. Well, sometimes it takes awhile to figure that out.

CHERYL. How long?

LORI. It took me three years to realize my husband and I had *no* chemistry.

CHERYL. Not helpful.

LORI. There must be *something* you like about him.

CHERYL. He's nice, seems smart, has no ego, likes *Lord of the Rings*. He asked me questions about myself. Most guys just talk about *themselves*. And he likes coffee.

LORI. Who doesn't? Last Tuesday I made my coffee with Red Bull instead of water. I got halfway to work before I realized I forgot my car.

CHERYL. I have no words for that.

LORI. How big are his feet?

CHERYL. I don't know. Why?

LORI. The bigger the feet, the bigger the...

CHERYL. Oh!

LORI. Birkenstocks.

CHERYL. Bye, Lori.

LORI. *(Imitating Arnold Schwarzenegger.)* "I'll be back."

*(**LORI** exits. **CHERYL** gets on her computer.)*

*(Lights up, stage left. **STAN** enters with coffee, followed by **DAVE**. **STAN** goes to his computer.)*

STAN. I'm so nervous.

DAVE. Don't be nervous. You have to be cool. If you're not cool, you'll lose her.

STAN. You're right, be cool. Wait, I've never been cool. How do I be cool?

DAVE. Just don't propose to her.

STAN. That's a lot to ask.

DAVE. And try to hold off on your goofy jokes.

STAN. My jokes are goofy?

DAVE. Well, they're just a little...

> *(Thinks.)*

Yeah, they're goofy.

STAN. Okay, no jokes.

> *(Looks at his computer.)*

Oh, hey, she signed in. She's waiting for me.

DAVE. Good luck. I'll be right here if you need me.

> *(**DAVE** stays. **STAN** gives him a look.)*

I'll just...be in the wine cellar.

> *(**DAVE** steps out. **STAN** hits a key on his computer.)*

CHERYL. Hi, Stan.

> *(**STAN** mouths several words but doesn't speak.)*

I think you're muted.

> *(**STAN** mouths more, gets animated.)*

You're muted. Hit the button lower left.

(**STAN** *mouths more, doesn't speak.*)

The mute button, lower left –

STAN. I'm just messing with you.

CHERYL. Wow, that was...semi-amusing.

STAN. Just "semi?" I was hoping for...

(**STAN** *freezes in place.*)

CHERYL. Stan?...

STAN. Movie theater...

(He freezes.)

CHERYL. You froze up.

STAN. Cranberries and bacon...

(He freezes.)

CHERYL. We've got a bad connection.

STAN. Got ya again.

CHERYL. Okay, now you're pushing it.

STAN. Sorry.

(To himself.)

Be cool.

CHERYL. You okay?

STAN. Yeah, yeah. Got my coffee, here. Folgers.

CHERYL. The richest kind.

STAN. Oh, well, the coffee might be rich, that doesn't mean *I* am. Just so you know.

CHERYL. O...kay?

STAN. So...how's your day going?

CHERYL. Good. I have a new client and I talked to them for awhile.

STAN. How do you get new clients? Referrals?

CHERYL. Mostly. This one was court appointed.

STAN. You must have a good reputation.

CHERYL. Oh, well, I mean, I enjoy what I do, I really care for my clients, and they seem to appreciate that.

STAN. Humble. So, what's the biggest challenge in your business?

CHERYL. Oh, umm...I'd say, when people try to take advantage of my clients, and I have to basically protect them, sometimes from family members, and it can get ugly.

STAN. I can imagine. So, how did you get into managing special needs trusts?

CHERYL. I have a special needs daughter.

STAN. Oh, okay. What's her name?

CHERYL. Jennifer. She's great.

STAN. Does she live with you?

CHERYL. No, I wanted her to live with me, but she wanted to be on her own. She's twenty-five. Has Down's Syndrome. High-functioning. She lives in a group home. It's not as bad as it sounds. Although it needs some renovating. She has friends there and seems to like it. I see her every week. She's...the light of my life.

STAN. She sounds sweet.

CHERYL. She is. So...you're a computer programmer.

STAN. Yeah, it's a living.

CHERYL. Do you have any hobbies?

STAN. I have a *Lord of the Rings* figurine collection –

DAVE. *(Offstage.)* NO!

STAN. Nope, nope, I do *not* have that.

CHERYL. A *Lord of the Rings* what?

STAN. I'm just a fan, that's all. Like you.

CHERYL. O...kay?

STAN. So, do you have any other kids?

CHERYL. A son. He's twenty-seven. Engineer at Lockheed, works in aerospace.

STAN. Good company. I've done some work for them.

CHERYL. Really? What kind of work?

STAN. Oh, just, programming, managing data, you know. What's your son's name?

CHERYL. Justin.

STAN. Do you see him much?

CHERYL. Not for a couple years.

STAN. Oh, well, kids today like a busy orbit.

CHERYL. He hasn't talked to me since his father died.

STAN. Oh, I'm sorry to hear that.

CHERYL. Yeah, I'm sorry, too. I miss him. It's been tough... You know, I should probably get going. I've got my own busy day. It's been nice talking to you.

STAN. Was it my jokes?

CHERYL. No, no, I just...got a lot of things to do.

STAN. So...can I see you again?

CHERYL. Oh, umm...

STAN. Lunch maybe?

CHERYL. Well...

STAN. Zoom lunch?

CHERYL. Why don't we just play it by ear.

STAN. Yeah, sure, okay. I'll send you my number. Have a good week.

CHERYL. You, too. Bye.

STAN. Bye.

> *(They hang up. Lights down, stage right.* **CHERYL** *exits.)*

What were you thinking? "Kids today like a busy orbit." Idiot.

DAVE. *(Entering.)* What happened?

STAN. It's over.

DAVE. Because you talked about your *Lord of the Rings* figurine collection. I told you.

STAN. Were you watching?

DAVE. For a minute. It was like watching the Hindenburg.

> *(He mimics an explosion.)*

STAN. A little encouragement?

DAVE. I'm just looking out for you. Do you like her?

STAN. Yeah. She's perfect.

DAVE. Well, then against my better judgement, go after her.

STAN. Yeah, you're right. I will.

> *(Abruptly exits, leaving* **DAVE**.*)*

DAVE. Okay, good talk.

> *(Lights down, stage left.* **DAVE** *exits. Lights up, stage right.* **CHERYL** *enters with* **LORI**.*)*

LORI. It's not the worst thing in the world. Eventually, you would have to tell him about your son.

CHERYL. Why?

LORI. Because that's what people do in a relationship.

CHERYL. We're not in a relationship.

LORI. Okay, well, what happened, happened. Was he weird about it?

CHERYL. No. He was nice and normal. I just reacted a little strongly.

LORI. Well, don't do that.

CHERYL. I just don't know if he's my type.

LORI. Last time I was somebody's type, I was giving blood.

CHERYL. Don't you have to have an attraction?

LORI. You want an attraction? Go to Disneyland.

CHERYL. I'm just not sure there's any romantic connection there.

LORI. Get him to dance.

CHERYL. Why?

LORI. You can tell what kind of moves a guy has when he dances. You'll be able to tell if you're compatible in the…

(Making bed squeaking noises.)

Eee ee eee ee eee ee.

CHERYL. A, that's ridiculous, B, how do I get him to dance?

LORI. You'll figure it out. What's the next step?

CHERYL. We might have a Zoom lunch.

LORI. Let him take you to lunch. My gosh, at least get a meal out of it.

CHERYL. I don't want to lead him on.

LORI. Why?

CHERYL. It's not right.

LORI. It's dating. There is no "right."

CHERYL. So encouraging.

LORI. Does Stan have any friends?

CHERYL. Dave. We should set you up.

LORI. What's he like?

CHERYL. I think he's the male version of you.

LORI. He sounds perfect.

CHERYL. I'll let you know what happens with Stan.

> *(Lights down, stage right.* **CHERYL** *and* **LORI** *exit.)*

(A week later.)

(Lights up, stage left. **STAN** *enters, on his phone.)*

DAVE. *(Enters on platform on his phone.)* You're waiting for *her* to call?

STAN. I'm not sure how we left it.

DAVE. Women don't call. I'd move on. You have any other prospects?

STAN. No, nothing yet...

(Looks at his phone.)

Wait...I'm back in.

DAVE. Back in where?

STAN. With Cheryl. She just texted me. It's a good thing. We're on for Zoom lunch.

DAVE. Zoom lunch? How is that a good thing?

STAN. It's the best I could do.

DAVE. You gotta get face to face. Otherwise you'll land in the friend zone. Have you ever been in the friend zone?

STAN. I haven't been in *any* zone.

DAVE. She tells you how perfect you are for *someone else*, and says things like, "You're like a brother to me."

(Shudders.)

Listen, you do *not* wanna be in the friend zone.

STAN. I'll keep you posted.

(Lights down, stage left. **STAN** *and* **DAVE** *exit.)*

(A few days later.)

(Lights up, stage right. **CHERYL** *enters, on her phone, with a sandwich on a plate, goes to her computer.)*

CHERYL. I've got a few minutes.

LORI. *(Enters on platform on her phone.)* Find out how much money he has.

CHERYL. I don't care about his money.

LORI. You are not well. Ask him what kind of a car he drives. That'll give you an idea.

CHERYL. You are relentless.

LORI. Look, you don't want him to be a deadbeat. You don't wanna have to take care of him in your old age. You want *him* to take care of *you.*

CHERYL. I'm not sure if I'll ever see him in person.

LORI. Let him take you to dinner. See if he eats with his mouth open. Deal breaker.

CHERYL. I gotta go.

*(***LORI*** exits.* **CHERYL** *logs in. Lights up, stage left.* **STAN** *enters with a sandwich on a plate,* **DAVE** *follows.)*

DAVE. Probe her.

STAN. What?

DAVE. Interrogate her. What is she after. Is it money? Find out her ulterior motive.

STAN. I don't think she has an ulterior –

DAVE. You don't need another woman after your money.

STAN. I think she has her own money.

DAVE. Get her to dance.

STAN. Why?

DAVE. You need to know what you're in for when you're about to do the horizontal mambo.

STAN. I don't know the mambo.

DAVE. Learn it. They have videos. Wait, are you still functioning...

(*A beat.*)

...down there?

STAN. Yeah! I mean it's been awhile, but probably.

DAVE. They have to know you can perform. You can take supplements, you know, that can help you with your...

(**DAVE** *makes elephant trumpeting sounds while raising his arm up and down, like an elephant trunk.*)

STAN. Yes, I'm aware.

DAVE. How does she look? Hot? Matronly? Like a nun? Sexy?

STAN. (*Getting on his computer.*) Umm...professional.

DAVE. Run. Just run. Run, run, run.

STAN. Why?

DAVE. Professional women are sharks.

STAN. No, they're not.

DAVE. Get on her bad side, she will chomp off your numchucks.

STAN. See ya.

DAVE. I'll be on the heli-pad.

(**DAVE** *exits.* **STAN** *hits a key on his computer.*)

STAN. *(Checking his breath.)* Why am I checking my breath?

CHERYL. Hi Stan. How are you?

STAN. *(Busted.)* Oh, hi, Cheryl. Got my lunch here, BLT. Life is good.

CHERYL. That's what *I'm* having. What are the odds?

STAN. We're meant for each other. We should get marrie –

DAVE. *(Offstage.)* NO!

STAN. *(Sings, covering.)*

   MARY HAD A LITTLE PIG.

     (Spoken.)

Singin' for my lunch. Anyhoo, how've you been?

CHERYL. *(Puzzled.)* Uhh, good, just working, keeping busy. I'm trying to customize an accounting program to track expenses so I can be a little more proactive.

STAN. Quickbooks, that's pretty easy. You want me to program something for you? I'm free.

     (**STAN** *hits a key. Music starts to play.**)

CHERYL. Thank you. You're very nice, but I have someone who can do it for me. Is that music?

STAN. Yeah, you like music?

CHERYL. Sure, I've been known to hit the dance floor. When I'm drunk.

STAN. *I'm* a pretty good dancer... Is something nobody ever told me.

---

* A license to produce *Love...or Best Offer* does not include a performance license for any third-party or copyrighted music. Licensees should create an original composition or use music in the public domain. For further information, please see the Music and Third-Party Materials Use Note on page iii.

CHERYL. That's a good song.

STAN. Shall we?

CHERYL. Why not?

(They dance in front of their computer cameras.)

STAN. This isn't weird, is it?

CHERYL. Totally. Hopefully, no one is watching.

STAN. I'm ready to bust a move. You ready for it?

CHERYL. You have to ask?

STAN. I learned this one in the Navy.

*(**STAN** mimes like he's putting on pants, wiggling his hips, pulling them from his ankles over his thighs.)*

CHERYL. You were in the Navy?

STAN. *Old* Navy. I bought these pants there.

CHERYL. Hey, as fun as this is, how long are we gonna keep doing it?

STAN. Big finish!

*(**STAN** finishes with his grand finale move, a high kick, then winces in pain. He hits a key. The music stops. They sit back down.)*

CHERYL. Are you okay?

STAN. *(Feeling pain.)* I think I pulled a groin muscle.

CHERYL. Oh, no.

STAN. I'll be fine. I'll ice it later.

CHERYL. O-kay. So...I didn't ask before, do you have kids?

STAN. No. And it's my biggest regret. I really wanted kids, but my wife...ex-wife, didn't.

CHERYL. Sorry to hear that.

STAN. What can you do. She was young and beautiful. She had other plans.

CHERYL. I hate those young, beautiful ones.

STAN. I know. I am *so* over them.

CHERYL. Apparently.

STAN. Oh, my gosh, that sounded horrible. No, no, you are very...nicely...proportioned... I'm flailing. Anyway, we got divorced. And now it's a little late for kids I'm afraid.

CHERYL. I don't know. You look like you still have a little spring in your step.

STAN. Well, these hips don't lie. Except for the artificial one. Anyhoo, I just don't see myself playing football in the backyard with my son at eighty-two.

CHERYL. Maybe, but you can play cribbage with him in the nursing home while icing your groin.

STAN. *(Chuckles.)* So, how's your daughter, Jennifer?

CHERYL. She's wonderful. She works at the Salvation Army, sorting clothes. It keeps her busy.

STAN. How does she like her group home?

CHERYL. She likes it. I wish they had an activity center. A place to socialize, play games, do crafts.

STAN. What do they have now?

CHERYL. Just a room with a TV. It seems like they could do more to provide more activities.

STAN. Have you talked to 'em about it?

CHERYL. Yeah, it's not in their budget right now.

STAN. Huh. What did you say was the name of the home?

CHERYL. Reagent Care.

STAN. *(He types something.)* I'd like to meet her some day.

CHERYL. Oh. Okay, well...let me think about that.

STAN. I mean, you know, no pressure, but...if it works out, great.

CHERYL. I wanted to tell you about my son. I kind of cut you off last time.

STAN. Oh, no, that's okay.

CHERYL. The reason he hasn't spoken to me for two years...well, he would tell you that I was really tough on him. He was very close to his father, who was kind of the buffer, and with his father gone he...didn't care to endure my scrutiny.

STAN. Do you feel you were too hard on him?

CHERYL. Maybe. But, I wanted him to be happy, to be successful, get married and have kids. My daughter doesn't wanna get married or have kids. I mean, I love my daughter, I'd do anything for her, but she has limitations, due to no fault of her own. And my son has *no* limitations, so I pushed him to be the best person he could be. And he does well, but he resents me for pushing him. I think he also resents losing the parent he was closest to.

STAN. He just needs some time. He'll come around.

CHERYL. Thanks for the therapy session.

STAN. That'll be four hundred dollars.

CHERYL. *(She smiles.)* So, Mr. Programmer. What do you program?

STAN. Well, one of the things I wrote is an algorithm that helps map out traffic patterns and population trends.

CHERYL. Oh, like Waze?

STAN. Something like that. The public uses it, but also municipalities rely on it to decide where to build or expand freeways and place traffic lights. It's also used by trucking and shipping companies to help with scheduling, maximizing efficiency, saving time, gas, stuff like that. It can also slice, dice and serrate julienned vegetables.

CHERYL. I need one of those. And they use it all over the country?

STAN. Yeah. And Canada, parts of Europe, Australia.

CHERYL. Wow. Impressive.

STAN. I'm good at helping others get where *they* wanna go, I just can't seem to get there myself.

CHERYL. You must be very successful. I bet you have a nice car.

STAN. Oh, I don't know. A car is a car. Do you like nice cars?

CHERYL. Oh, no, I just thought that you must be doing well.

STAN. I do okay. Are you looking for a guy that does well?

CHERYL. What? No, no, I mean, someone who has a decent job or is retired comfortably.

STAN. Would you say that you're content...financially?

CHERYL. Fairly... Are you?

STAN. Yeah. Oh, boy, I'm sorry, I didn't mean to get so personal.

CHERYL. Oh, no, don't worry about it.

STAN. Let me make it up to you. Can I take you to a, sitting-at-the-same-table, dinner?

CHERYL. You don't have to do that.

STAN. How about drinks, then?

CHERYL. How about Zoom drinks? Next weekend?

STAN. *(Defeated.)* Sure. Zoom drinks. See you then. Take care.

CHERYL. Bye.

> *(Hangs up, mocking herself.)*

"I bet you drive a nice car. I just thought you must be doing well." Idiot.

> *(Lights down, stage right.* **CHERYL** *exits with her sandwich.* **DAVE** *enters, stage left.)*

DAVE. How'd it go? You gonna finally see her in person?

STAN. We're having "Zoom drinks."

DAVE. Buddy, only Zoom dating leads to one thing.

STAN. Zoom sex?

DAVE. No! The friend zone! Which is where you are.

STAN. I know. How do I get out?

DAVE. You gotta go with something big. It's time for the Hail Mary.

STAN. You're right. Let's hire ten airplanes to fly all over town pulling banners that say, "Stan Loves Cheryl."

DAVE. That's a horrible idea.

STAN. Right. It's not big enough... Hey, you know that group home her daughter is in?

DAVE. Yeah, you mentioned it.

STAN. Let's put a million dollars into renovating it.

DAVE. I said big, not that big.

STAN. I drove by it. It needs a rec room and a pool.

DAVE. Are you stalking her daughter?

STAN. I just drove by. Will you do that for me, please?

DAVE. You're the boss.

STAN. And I want it to be anonymous. I don't want anyone to know who paid for it.

DAVE. I thought you wanted to impress her.

STAN. I do. I just need to figure out when to tell her.

DAVE. You know that's how you got in trouble with your first wife, right?

STAN. I know, and I'm not gonna make that mistake again.

DAVE. I hope you know what you're doing.

STAN. I have no idea what I'm doing.

> *(Lights down, stage left.* **STAN** *and* **DAVE** *exit.* **STAN** *takes his sandwich.)*

(A week later.)

(Lights up, stage right. **CHERYL** *enters with a glass of red wine, followed by* **LORI**.*)*

LORI. You're doing "Zoom drinks?"

CHERYL. Yes, and I'm going with a Napa cabernet.

LORI. Are you ever gonna see him in person?

CHERYL. I don't know.

LORI. So you don't really care about him romantically.

CHERYL. I mean, I look at him like a friend.

LORI. Whoa. Does *he* know that?

CHERYL. I don't know. It's just...he doesn't even come close to Steve.

LORI. Oh. My. Grundies! You're making excuses. Look, I know you loved Steve more than anything, but Steve wasn't perfect. You said it yourself, he wasn't entirely honest about a few things.

CHERYL. I know, I know.

LORI. Stan seems like a trustworthy guy.

CHERYL. He is. It's just that...the last call got a little weird, the whole money thing.

LORI. Well, maybe he's broke. Maybe *he's* after *your* money.

CHERYL. I don't have that much.

LORI. Yeah, you do. You do well with your business and you got the life insurance payout.

CHERYL. I'm okay, but not so okay that someone would wanna go after it.

*(***CHERYL*** goes to her computer.)*

LORI. Look, you need to tell him how you feel, or don't feel, about him. As for me, I like my feelings just as I like my water; bottled up. But in your case, be honest, don't lead him on.

CHERYL. "Be honest?" That's new.

LORI. Relish it. You might never hear it again.

CHERYL. Inspiring.

LORI. If you need me, I'll be in the liquor cabinet.

>*(**LORI** exits. Lights up, stage left. **STAN** enters, and goes to his computer.)*

CHERYL. *(To herself.)* This'll be fun. "Hey, Stan, how's your day going? Really? Great. Let's stop Zooming each other."

>*(Hits a key on her computer.)*

And here we go.

>*(**STAN** puts on a goofy mask. He hits a computer key.)*

STAN. Hi Cheryl.

CHERYL. Hi Stan. You're...wearing a mask.

STAN. Oh, it's an AR filter. Hit a key, it makes your face look funny.

CHERYL. Mission accomplished.

STAN. I'll take it off.

>*(Fakes hitting a key.)*

There.

>*(The mask is still on his face.)*

CHERYL. Still on.

STAN. Oh, shoot.

> *(Fakes hitting a key.)*

How about now?

CHERYL. Still on.

STAN. *(Takes mask off.)* How about now?

CHERYL. *(Laughs.)* Have you ever thought about being a comedian?

STAN. No.

CHERYL. Good.

STAN. How can you say that? I'm giving you my best material.

CHERYL. Oh, I'm sure you are.

STAN. You'll come around.

CHERYL. Uh huh. So, how have you been?

STAN. Good, good. I've been looking forward to our Zoom drink all week. I'm all set here with my glass of wine.

> *(He holds up a large Big Gulp cup with a straw.* Takes a swig.)*

CHERYL. *(Laughs.)* You are such a goof.

STAN. Thank you... So, I've been thinking about you a lot and I wanted to tell you something.

CHERYL. Sure, sure, but first can I be honest with you about something?

STAN. *That* doesn't sound good.

CHERYL. Stan, you're a good guy.

STAN. Oh, no.

---

* A license to produce *Love...or Best Offer* does not include a license to publicly display any branded logos or trademarked images. Licensees must acquire rights for any logos and/or images or create their own.

CHERYL. I'm not sure what your thoughts are on our relationship. I just don't wanna lead you on.

STAN. Please, lead me on.

CHERYL. I can't do that. You're too good of a person. I just don't think I'm right for you.

STAN. I do.

CHERYL. I mean, you're like a...

STAN. *(To himself.)* Oh, no.

CHERYL. You're like a brother to me.

STAN. *(Groans.)* Ahhh.

CHERYL. It's just that, I'm worried about your expectations, and I'm afraid I'm gonna let you down.

STAN. *(Feels his chest.)* I think I'm having a heart attack.

CHERYL. You are!?

STAN. No, I'm just trying to get sympathy. Is it working?

CHERYL. I'm sorry.

STAN. So...what does this mean? Do we not talk anymore?

CHERYL. Well, that's up to you. I enjoy talking to you, and I'd be happy to stay in touch as friends.

STAN. *(In pain.)* Oh, the "F" word.

> *(Groans.)*

Ahh...okay, okay, breathe...

> *(Takes a deep breath.)*

Alright, okay. If, ahh...if that's your best offer, I'll...give it a try.

CHERYL. Thanks. Was there something you wanted to tell me?

STAN. No. I just missed you, that's all.

(Looks at phone.)

Oh, that's Dave. I'll call him back.

CHERYL. No, I'll let you go.

STAN. We'll talk.

CHERYL. Okay, bye.

STAN. Bye.

>*(Lights down, stage right.* **CHERYL** *exits.* **STAN** *answers his phone.)*

I am *deep* in the friend zone.

DAVE. *(Enters on platform on his phone.)* It happens to the best of us. My girlfriend just dumped *me*.

STAN. Sorry to hear that.

DAVE. Oh, no, it's okay. She was always complaining that I never *listen* to her...or something like that, I don't know.

STAN. Cheryl said it was okay to keep in touch. As a friend.

DAVE. Buddy, buddy, maybe you should just cut your losses on this one.

STAN. I can't. I love her.

DAVE. Do not say that. You don't love her.

STAN. I think I do.

DAVE. I'm gonna set you up with my therapist. As a patient, not a date.

STAN. No need. I'm gonna muscle this one out myself. She'll see the light.

DAVE. You're further gone than I thought. Did you tell her about your million dollar renovation to the group home?

STAN. No.

DAVE. Good. I'll cancel it.

STAN. No, don't.

DAVE. You're just throwing your money away.

STAN. No, I'm not. It's for a great cause. I've done a lot of research on the home, they deserve it, and frankly, I was never able to do anything for *my* kids.

DAVE. You don't *have* kids.

STAN. I'm saying, I might as well do something for someone *else's* kids.

DAVE. Someone else that you're not dating.

STAN. We're doing the renovation. I'd like it done quickly, and I don't want her to know I paid for it. Okay, buddy?

DAVE. It's *your* money.

> *(Lights down, stage left. **STAN** and **DAVE** exit. Lights up, stage right. **CHERYL** enters, followed by **LORI**.)*

LORI. Being honest with Stan was the right thing to do. Maybe.

CHERYL. He took it better than I thought.

LORI. At least he didn't cry.

CHERYL. I feel bad. I like him.

LORI. Yeah, you tend to like the people you put in the "friend zone."

CHERYL. It sounds like the "Twilight Zone."

LORI. It is. For *men*. You just have to make sure he knows you're friends. Otherwise, he's gonna keep workin' on you like a colony of ants on a warm Snickers bar.

> *(Dreaming of a Snickers bar.)*

CHERYL. Are you hungry?

LORI. Starving. Anyway, I have some other prospects for you.

CHERYL. *(Groans.)* Ohh. So soon?

LORI. No time to waste. You need to get back up in the saddle.

CHERYL. The saddle is chafing my butt.

> *(Lights down, stage right.* **CHERYL** *and* **LORI** *exit.)*

(A few weeks later.)

*(Lights up, stage left. **STAN** enters, on his phone.)*

STAN. My ex-wife has been texting me.

DAVE. *(Enters on platform on his phone.)* Cruella DeJill?

STAN. I think she just prefers, "Jill."

DAVE. What does she want?

STAN. I don't know. I guess to talk. I haven't texted her back.

DAVE. Probably wondering when she gets her thirty million.

STAN. I don't think so. The lawyers update her on that.

DAVE. Hey, what's the deal with Lori?

STAN. Cheryl's friend?

DAVE. Yeah. What is she like?

STAN. I think she's a lot like you.

DAVE. Sweet. It sounds like she's hot.

STAN. So...you're saying that *you're* hot?

DAVE. Well, I would say that I'm definitely within the zip code, yes.

STAN. I'm surprised you still wanna date. It doesn't sound like you're that fond of women.

DAVE. I love women. Especially the ones that have a deep love for *me*.

STAN. Oh, hey, that's Cheryl. Gotta go.

*(Lights up, stage right. **CHERYL** enters, on her phone.)*

DAVE. See ya.

*(**DAVE** exits. **STAN** answers the phone.)*

STAN. Hey, Cheryl, how have you been?

CHERYL. Good. Busy. You?

STAN. Can't complain. Well, I could, but at least I'm still above ground...

    (He laughs.)

Oh, that was in poor taste. I'm sorry.

CHERYL. Stan, I just wanna make sure that you're okay with being friends.

STAN. *(In pain.)* Yeah, I'm okay.

CHERYL. Thanks. I met someone on SilverSingles.

STAN. *(To himself.)* Oh, crap.

CHERYL. *(Didn't hear him.)* I'm sorry, what?

STAN. *(Busted, covering.)* Oh, snap... That is *so* great.

CHERYL. Maybe I shouldn't have said anything.

STAN. No, no, that's what friends are for. To talk about stuff. And that definitely falls in the "stuff" category.

CHERYL. How are you doing? Have you met anyone online?

STAN. Oh, well, I guess I'm not really looking.

CHERYL. You want me to help you find someone?

STAN. *(Groans.)* Ahhh.

CHERYL. I can tell this is uncomfortable for you.

STAN. No, no, we're here. We might as well land it.

CHERYL. So, this guy I went out with is a dentist. His name is Jim.

STAN. Oh, okay, you're just gonna go right ahead there and tell me all about Jim.

CHERYL. You're right. That's inappropriate. I'm sorry.

STAN. Nope. Go ahead. We're friends.

> *(To himself.)*

Dangit.

CHERYL. Well, he's been practicing for thirty-five years. He specializes in root canals.

STAN. "Root canals." Wow.

CHERYL. Apparently, he really enjoys it.

STAN. Really? Well, that's...disturbing... You know what, I forgot, I have a thing.

CHERYL. "A thing?"

STAN. Yeah, I gotta go and do this thing with the deal and the...people.

CHERYL. Oh, okay, well, I'll let you go.

STAN. You know what, I feel like I'm kind of smothering you. I'm gonna give you some space.

CHERYL. Oh. Okay.

STAN. Take your time and call me when, and if...you feel like it.

CHERYL. Okay.

STAN. Take care.

CHERYL. Bye.

STAN. *(Hangs up.)* That was painful.

> *(Lights down, stage left.* **STAN** *exits.* **CHERYL** *speed dials* **LORI**.*)*

CHERYL. *(To herself.)* Wow, that just went sideways... Of course it did. What were you expecting?

LORI. *(Enters on platform on her phone.)* How's the dentist?

CHERYL. He's okay. He's going to a root canal convention this week.

LORI. Sounds like a shindig. Is Stan okay with the dentist?

CHERYL. I'm gonna go with...not entirely.

LORI. Just cut him loose. You know he cares for you. This can not be healthy for him.

CHERYL. You're right. I just don't wanna hurt him.

LORI. Just pull off the bandaid. In a few weeks, the oozing will stop.

CHERYL. Okay, I'll do it. It's for the best.

> (*Lights down, stage right.* **CHERYL** *and* **LORI** *exit.*)

(A few weeks later.)

(Lights up, stage left. **STAN** *enters, followed by* **DAVE**.*)*

DAVE. So, what's the next step?

STAN. I decided to date other people.

DAVE. "Date other people" implies that you're *currently* dating someone.

STAN. I decided to date *people*.

DAVE. Good for you. Anyone you have in mind?

STAN. Someone in the office.

DAVE. Oh, no. Absolutely not. That did *not* work out last time.

STAN. I have to do *something*. I can't get Cheryl off my mind.

DAVE. Get a puppy.

STAN. I don't want a puppy. I want Cheryl.

DAVE. Do not date anyone in the office.

STAN. Too late.

(Looks at his phone.)

Oh, hey, it's Cheryl. I gotta take this.

DAVE. *(Groans.)* Ahh.

*(***DAVE*** exits. Lights up, stage right.* **CHERYL** *enters, on her phone.* **STAN** *answers his phone.)*

STAN. Stan Jensen reporting for duty.

CHERYL. So formal. How've you been?

STAN. I'm good. How's the dentist?

CHERYL. Oh, he's fine.

STAN. *(Makes tooth drill sound.)* Zzzzzzzzzzzzzzz zzzzzzzzz...

(No response from **CHERYL**.*)*

That's a tooth drilling sound –

CHERYL. Got it.

STAN. So... I met someone.

CHERYL. *(Conflicted.)* Really? That's...great. Tell me about her.

STAN. Well, she's smart and attractive, like you. She's a lawyer, so if we ever get married, I'll be sure to lose another house. She has two kids, and two grandkids.

CHERYL. Wow. She sounds impressive.

STAN. Yeah, she is.

CHERYL. Did you meet her online?

STAN. No, she was the in-house counsel on the sale of my...

(Reverses course.)

You know, it was just a little project. Nothing big. She was helpful.

CHERYL. What was the project?

STAN. I could tell you, but then I'd have to kill you.

(Laughs, then realizing.)

Sorry, that was bad. Delete that.

CHERYL. I notice you make a lot of murder jokes.

STAN. Why do I do that? I couldn't hurt a fly, unless it flew into my windshield and splattered all over, but even then I'd try to revive it with CPR.

(Makes tiny CPR motion with sounds.)

Ee ee ee ee. Clear! I'll stop talking.

CHERYL. I'm very happy for you.

STAN. Thanks... I gotta be honest. It took awhile to get over you. I mean you really had me, and when you said you wanted to date other people and keep me as a friend, it was tough for me. But life is tough, you know. And adversity makes you stronger. So, thank you for throwing adversity into my face. Hard. Really hard.

CHERYL. Umm...sure. I, ahh...I'm glad you found someone.

STAN. Thanks.

CHERYL. Is it weird if we keep talking as friends?

STAN. I don't know.

CHERYL. Maybe you're right. Maybe we should take a break for awhile.

STAN. If that's what you want.

CHERYL. Yeah, I think it's probably best for both of us.

STAN. Yeah, sure, okay.

CHERYL. It was good talking to you. It always is. Take care.

(*She exits.*)

STAN. You, too. Bye.

(*Lights down, stage right.* **DAVE** *enters, stage left.*)

DAVE. (*On his phone.*) I'll call you back.

(*Hangs up, to* **STAN**.)

You're dating Janet in legal?!

STAN. She seems to get me.

DAVE. Of course she does, she's your lawyer. She knows how much money you have.

STAN. (*As he exits.*) She really likes me.

DAVE. *(Following **STAN** out.)* Because she's made a ton of money off you.

*(Lights down, stage left. **STAN** and **DAVE** exit. Lights up, stage right. **CHERYL** enters, on her phone.)*

CHERYL. It kinda hurt. I didn't think it would.

LORI. *(Enters on platform on her phone.)* You knew he was gonna start dating someone eventually.

CHERYL. I think I have feelings for him.

LORI. It'll go away. In a few days, you'll realize it's for the best and move on.

CHERYL. Yeah, maybe. I just...did I mess up? I mean, did I lose Stan forever?

LORI. What, do you want him to be on hold for you in case your other dates don't work out?

CHERYL. That sounds awful. Am I a horrible person?

LORI. You're like everyone else. You want what you can't have, no matter if you want it or not.

CHERYL. That's so cynical.

LORI. It's a cynical world.

CHERYL. Stan isn't cynical. He's the most sincere, nicest guy I've ever met.

LORI. There are lots of nice guys. Allegedly.

CHERYL. If I didn't know you better, I'd think you don't like men.

LORI. I love men. Especially the ones with a high esteem. Of me. Back to Stan.

CHERYL. He's kind-hearted. I'm a sucker for kind-hearted. And he's funny in an awkward, goofy way. And he's such a nerd. It's kind of charming. Reminds me of my son.

LORI. Have you heard from Justin?

CHERYL. I send him texts but nothing back.

LORI. Give him time.

CHERYL. Yeah...Stan's gone. Guys don't keep women friends when they find a girlfriend. Wow, I didn't think I'd feel this way.

LORI. You made a decision. You traded up from a programmer to a dentist.

CHERYL. I think I made a mistake.

LORI. You'll get over it.

> *(Lights down, stage right.* **CHERYL** *and* **LORI** *exit. Lights up, stage left.* **STAN** *enters, followed by* **DAVE**.*)*

STAN. I'm telling you, Janet is different.

DAVE. How is your legal counsel any different than your ex-wife?

STAN. First of all, she's much smarter.

DAVE. Would Janet be dating you if you didn't have so much money?

STAN. Yes, of course she would.

DAVE. Stan, it's me.

STAN. No, she wouldn't.

DAVE. You still talking to Cheryl?

STAN. We're kind of taking a break.

DAVE. Okay, you've got the upper hand. She thinks you're happy in your relationship. Make her keep thinking that. She'll want you more. Give her a few months, then call her.

STAN. Why can't I just be honest?

DAVE. No, no, no, no, no! Honesty does not work!

STAN. *(As he exits.)* Bye, Dave.

DAVE. *(Following him out.)* I'm just being honest.

      (Lights down, stage left. **STAN** *and* **DAVE** *exit.)*

(A few months later.)

(Lights up, stage right. **CHERYL** *enters, on her phone.)*

CHERYL. I'm gonna be honest with him.

LORI. *(Enters on platform, on phone, mirroring* **DAVE.***)* No, no, no, no, no! Honesty does not work!

CHERYL. He deserves it. Look, *he's* a nice guy. And he's honest with *me.*

LORI. That's just temporary. He's gonna break. They all do. He's a man. It's in their DNA. Just watch. You'll be having dinner, "Hey Cheryl, did I mention that I have *sixteen kids*?" "No, you didn't, Stan." "Yeah, funny thing, I donated sperm in college. They found out where I live and they're all moving in next week."

CHERYL. Did that happen to you?

LORI. *Yes!*

CHERYL. *(Looking at her phone.)* Stan's calling. I gotta go.

LORI. Good luck.

> *(***LORI*** *exits. Lights up, stage left.* **STAN** *enters.* **CHERYL** *and* **STAN** *on the phone.)*

CHERYL. Hey Stan, it's been awhile.

STAN. *(Looks at his watch.)* Eight weeks, three days and two hours.

> *(He laughs, lying.)*

I haven't been keeping track.

CHERYL. So...how is everything?

STAN. Good, good. I've been traveling. My girlfriend and I went to my winery in Napa.

CHERYL. You went *where*?

STAN. *(Correcting himself.)* To *a* winery in Napa.

CHERYL. Oh, well, that must have been nice.

STAN. Yeah, it was good. So, what's new with you?

CHERYL. Well, they're building an activity center for my daughter's group home.

STAN. Really?

CHERYL. Yeah, they're almost done. And they're putting in a swimming pool. I don't know where they found the money, but I'm not complaining.

STAN. That's great. Hopefully, Jennifer will enjoy it.

CHERYL. Oh, my gosh, she is thrilled! Everyone there is thrilled.

STAN. I'm glad. They deserve it.

CHERYL. I was wondering...look if you're happy with your girlfriend, I understand. I just...I think I made a mistake.

STAN. What kind of mistake?

CHERYL. With *you*. That sounded bad. The mistake was asking you to be a friend instead of...dating.

STAN. So...things aren't going well with your boyfriend?

CHERYL. We broke up.

STAN. *(Celebrating.)* Sorry to hear that.

CHERYL. We just...weren't meant for each other.

STAN. So...you're available?

CHERYL. You know what, if you're happy, I don't wanna get in the way.

STAN. What made you change your mind?

CHERYL. I don't know, I just...miss you.

STAN. I miss you, too.

CHERYL. Are you happy with her?

STAN. Happy?... It's ahh...complicated.

CHERYL. Look, I shouldn't have said anything. It was wrong.

STAN. No, no, I'm listening.

CHERYL. Well, if things don't work out with your girlfriend, let me know. I'll wait to hear from you, and if I don't, I wish you all the best. Take care.

STAN. Bye.

> *(He hits speed dial.)*

CHERYL. Congratulations. You are sooooo good at losing people...Sarcasm!

> *(Lights down, stage right.* **CHERYL** *exits.)*

STAN. Cheryl wants to get back together.

DAVE. *(Enters on platform on his phone.)* Because she knows you have money.

STAN. No, that's not it. She said she didn't know who paid for the renovation.

DAVE. And you believe her?

STAN. Yes.

DAVE. What happened to Janet in legal?

STAN. She wants to take a break. I don't think she cares for my sense of humor.

DAVE. Shocking.

STAN. What should I do about Cheryl?

DAVE. I would be very careful. You're vulnerable right now.

STAN. I'm gonna call her back and tell her how I feel.

DAVE. Oh, feelings are so overrated.

STAN. *(Starts to exit.)* She gave me an opening. I'm not gonna gamble on this one.

DAVE. May the force be with you.

STAN. *(On his exit.)* Yes, my *precious*!

(Lights down, stage left. **STAN** *and* **DAVE** *exit.)*

(One day later.)

*(Lights up, stage right. **CHERYL** enters, followed by **LORI**.)*

CHERYL. He seems happy with his new girlfriend. Are we too old to have "boyfriends"? Shouldn't it be "manfriend."

LORI. Well, *most* of them are *boys*.

CHERYL. Anyway, he's happy. And I screwed up. The more I talk to him, the more I like him.

LORI. You might wanna take another run at him.

CHERYL. Why?

LORI. You know the renovation to the group home?

CHERYL. Yeah, it's amazing.

LORI. Stan paid for it.

CHERYL. He what?

LORI. He donated a million dollars for the renovation.

CHERYL. No, no, it was some big donor.

LORI. Yeah, the donor was Stan.

CHERYL. Stan doesn't have that kind of money.

LORI. Yes, he does. And a lot more where that came from. He recently sold off a division of his company for a hundred million dollars, plus stock options. And that's just a *division*.

CHERYL. What? No, he's a programmer.

LORI. Yeah, he is. He developed some sort of traffic algorithm that he sold for a *hundred million dollars, plus stock options*. Oh, did I mention he owns a winery in Napa?

CHERYL. How do you know all this?

LORI. Google. I also know the bookkeeper at the group home. She told me in confidence the company that donated the money was Stan's company. I *told* her I wouldn't *tell* anyone, and that I'd tell my *friends* not to tell anyone.

CHERYL. Why didn't he tell me?

LORI. Why didn't you Google him?

CHERYL. You think he doesn't trust me?

LORI. Maybe. There's more. He dedicated the renovation to Steve.

CHERYL. My husband?

LORI. There's a plaque on it and everything with his name.

CHERYL. What was he thinking?

LORI. They don't always think with their brains. Sometimes they think with their...

CHERYL. Oh!

LORI. Little brains.

CHERYL. *(Looks at her phone.)* Stan is calling again.

LORI. What are you gonna do?

CHERYL. I don't know. I used to be indecisive, but now I'm not so sure.

LORI. *(Puzzled by her statement.)* Take the call. Do you have any Snickers?

CHERYL. In the pantry, behind the Metamucil.

LORI. Oh, a two-fer.

> *(**LORI** exits. Lights up, stage left. **STAN** enters, on his phone. **CHERYL** answers her phone.)*

CHERYL. Hi, Stan.

STAN. Hey, Cheryl. How's everything?

CHERYL. Well, a couple things have changed since we last talked, yesterday.

STAN. Really? Like what?

CHERYL. Well, I just found out that *you* were the one who donated the money for the renovation on the group home.

STAN. *(Disappointed.)* Oh, boy.

CHERYL. Why didn't you tell me?

STAN. I wanted it to be anonymous.

CHERYL. Why would you spend a million dollars on a renovation to my daughter's group home?

STAN. Because it's a worthy cause.

CHERYL. Did you do this to get into my grundies?

STAN. I have no idea what that is.

CHERYL. What are you expecting from me?

STAN. Nothing. I just thought the addition would be a good thing, and that your daughter might be happy about it.

CHERYL. She is happy. I am, too. "Deeds will not be less valiant because they are unpraised."

STAN. *(In ecstasy.)* Lord of the Rings.

CHERYL. Why didn't you tell me you were rich?

STAN. Would you like me more if you knew I had money?

CHERYL. Well, no, but...

STAN. So, it shouldn't matter then, right?

CHERYL. But it's part of who you are.

STAN. Is it? I mean, I think you have a pretty good idea who I am.

CHERYL. Did you think I would glom on to you for your money?

STAN. You don't seem like that kind of person, but I don't know.

CHERYL. I guess you don't know me very well then, do you?

STAN. I might be able to know you better if you would ever let me see you in person.

CHERYL. Have I been dishonest with you?

STAN. I don't think so.

CHERYL. You, "don't *think* so?"

STAN. Why are you pushing me away? What are you afraid of?

CHERYL. I gotta go.

> *(Lights down, stage right.* **CHERYL** *exits.)*

STAN. Wait, no, I just...

> *(She's gone.)*

That did *not* go well.

> *(Hits speed dial, to himself.)*

How is that a bad thing? How is spending a million bucks on a renovation –

DAVE. *(Enters on platform on his phone.)* What's up?

STAN. It's over.

DAVE. You've said that before. What happened?

STAN. Cheryl found out I donated the money for the renovation.

DAVE. I didn't tell anyone.

STAN. I know.

DAVE. Was she appreciative?

STAN. Sort of. She doesn't care that I have money. Which is *so hot!*

DAVE. It's always about money.

STAN. I don't know. It seems like it's a turn off to her.

DAVE. Money? A turn off? Can you hear yourself?

> (*Lights down, stage left.* **STAN** *and* **DAVE** *exit. Lights up, stage right.* **CHERYL** *enters, followed by* **LORI**.)

CHERYL. Why wouldn't he tell me he was rich?

LORI. Well, maybe he has trust issues since his ex-wife took him for thirty million.

CHERYL. Thirty mill – how do you know that?

LORI. I know someone at the courthouse. I *told* her I wouldn't *tell* anyone. Anyway, didn't you say that money doesn't matter to you?

CHERYL. It doesn't.

LORI. You need to see a doctor.

CHERYL. It's not about money, it's about honesty.

LORI. "Honesty." Sounds like you're projecting your husband onto Stan.

CHERYL. Stan doesn't trust me.

LORI. Trust *you*? You don't trust *him* enough to actually meet him in person.

CHERYL. Stop it with the logic... I just don't think I'm ready.

LORI. Ready for what?

CHERYL. To be vulnerable again, okay? To get my heart broken again. To just...wanna die. I can't do that again.

LORI. So, it's fear that's keeping you away from him. News flash, love is dangerous, but you're a tough person, and, yeah, you might fall in love and get hurt again, but it's better to love and lose that love...*(Flailing.)*...than to not love, and then to not lose the love you lost – you know what I mean.

CHERYL. I'm just not ready to replace my husband.

LORI. You don't replace him. You *honor* him with all the great memories you have with him, including your two great kids.

CHERYL. Yeah, well that's the thing. I lost my son, too. And *that* I did on my own.

LORI. He'll find his way back.

CHERYL. *(Not convinced.)* Yeah.

LORI. You know I love you, right?

CHERYL. Yeah.

LORI. You had a great husband. Unlike mine.

CHERYL. Your husband wasn't that bad.

LORI. Really? My doctor said I could no longer touch anything alcoholic, so I *divorced* him.

CHERYL. Yeah, I remember.

LORI. My ex-husband is the reason God created the middle finger.

CHERYL. Okay, okay, I get it, and your point is? ...

LORI. Your biggest hurdle is you. If you wanna heal, you have to pick yourself up, take the risk and maybe endure some pain. And don't call me until you do.

> *(Starts to exit.)*

CHERYL. I hate you so much.

LORI. *(Over her shoulder.)* Love you.

     (Lights down, stage right. **LORI** *and* **CHERYL** *exit.)*

(A week later.)

(Lights up, stage left. **STAN** *enters on his phone.)*

STAN. Jill wants to get back together.

DAVE. *(Enters on platform on his phone.)* Your ex-wife? The witch?

STAN. She's not a witch. More like a Wiccan. And she's just misunderstood. She wants to call off the final settlement.

DAVE. Why? She has the money *and* the pool boy. I mean, you're a catch and everything, but why?

STAN. The pool boy left her.

DAVE. Well, that's karma.

STAN. She says she misses my sense of humor.

DAVE. Has she heard your jokes?

STAN. The point is, she feels she made a mistake. She says she still loves me.

DAVE. What about the thirty million?

STAN. She'll call it off. I won't have to pay it.

DAVE. Take it. Take it now. Don't even think about it. I mean, she's a horrible person, people think you're her father, but she's hot, and you get your thirty million back.

STAN. I don't know if I could live with her again.

DAVE. Put her in the guest house.

STAN. What if it's a ploy to come back and extract *more* money from me?

DAVE. It probably is, but we'll cross that bridge when we get to it.

STAN. What about Cheryl?

DAVE. I thought that was over.

STAN. It's *not* over, until the...

> (*Thinks.*)

...full-figured lady sings.

> (**STAN** *hits speed dial on his phone.*)

DAVE. Gotta love that guy.

> (**DAVE** *exits. Lights up stage right.* **CHERYL** *enters, on her phone.*)

CHERYL. Stan?

STAN. Cheryl. Okay, now before you say anything. I just wanna apologize for not being honest with you about the renovation.

CHERYL. I guess you had your reason. I just wish you could trust me.

STAN. I do. And I need your advice on something.

CHERYL. Okay, what is it?

STAN. I got a call from my ex-wife.

CHERYL. The one that got thirty million in the divorce?

STAN. How do you know about that?

CHERYL & STAN. Lori.

STAN. She wants to get back together.

CHERYL. What did you tell her?

STAN. That's what I wanted to ask *you*. What *should* I tell her?

CHERYL. Stan, I can't speak for you. What's in your heart?

STAN. *You* are.

CHERYL. I care for you, I really do. I'm just not sure it'll work. I'm kind of a mess right now. I'm dealing with a lot of stuff. I still haven't gotten over the...

    (Gets a phone call.)

Oh, it's my son. I'm sorry, can you hold for a minute?

STAN. Sure.

CHERYL. *(Clicks to other call.)* Justin?... Are you okay, what's wrong?... Stan Jensen? Yeah, I know Stan... He what?... Really?... At Lockheed?... You talked to him?... What did he... He did?... How did you?... Yes, of course. I just...I miss you, and I'm really sorry how it all...lunch?... You wanna have?...

    (Emotional, fighting back tears.)

Yes...yes, I would... I would like that very much... That sounds great, hon... Thank you for calling. I'm looking forward to seeing you. Bye.

    (Struck with emotion, **CHERYL** *clicks over to* **STAN**.*)*

STAN. Cheryl?... Are you there?

CHERYL. Yeah.

STAN. Everything okay? You wanna call me back?

CHERYL. No, no, I can talk.

STAN. How's your son?

CHERYL. Good, good. He wants to see me. He wants to talk.

STAN. That's great. Isn't it?

CHERYL. Yeah, it's great. It's wonderful. Turns out he saw a presentation the other day at Lockheed on a new aerospace simulator.

STAN. Oh, yeah, I heard about that.

CHERYL. Maybe because *you* were the presenter.

STAN. Oh, yeah, right. Turns out your son was there. Who knew?

CHERYL. Really?

STAN. Justin is a great kid.

CHERYL. Well, he's certainly impressed with *you*.

STAN. I'm glad you're gonna see him.

CHERYL. Sounds like you put in a good word for me.

STAN. I do what I can.

CHERYL. Would you, ahh...would you like to go out to dinner sometime?

STAN. Like a Zoom dinner?

CHERYL. No, a real dinner, in a restaurant.

STAN. Huzzah!

> *(Catches himself.)*

I mean, yeah, that would be nice. When?

CHERYL. Friday?

STAN. Great. I'll pick you up. Wait, I don't know where you live.

CHERYL. I'll text you my address.

STAN. I'm looking forward to it. So, what do I tell my ex-wife?

CHERYL. Tell her you have a date with me on Friday.

STAN. Yes, ma-lady.

CHERYL. See you then.

> *(**CHERYL** smiles. **STAN** hits speed dial.)*

STAN. *(Dancing, singing.)*

> I AM HAVIN' DINNER WITH MA-LA-DY,
> AND I AM GONNA SEE HER IN PER-SON.

CHERYL. Still here!

STAN. Dangit!

> *(**STAN** hits a button on his phone. Lights down, stage right. **CHERYL** exits.)*

DAVE. *(Enters on platform on his phone.)* What's the verdict?

STAN. I'm back in! I'm back in! I am *so*. *Back*. *In*!

DAVE. So...are you back in?

STAN. *Yes!*

DAVE. I'm happy for you. I really am. Who are you back in with?

STAN. Cheryl!

DAVE. Right, right, Cheryl. Well, that's good. She deserves someone who put a million bucks into her daughter's home.

STAN. It's not about the – you know what, I'm happy. Happier than I've been in a long time. I mean, I get to see her. In person. Sure it took months to get here, but think of the possibilities.

DAVE. I love your optimism. And I'm happy that you're happy. Now *you* need to set *me* up with someone.

STAN. I have just the person for you.

> *(Lights down, stage left. **STAN** and **DAVE** exit.)*

(Five days later.)

(Lights up, stage right. **CHERYL** *enters, on her phone.)*

LORI. *(Enters on platform on her phone.)* That is great that you're meeting with your son.

CHERYL. I am so happy.

LORI. How did he get Justin to call you?

CHERYL. I don't know, but he did.

LORI. So, Stan is back in the picture?

CHERYL. He's picking me up in a few minutes.

LORI. You just broke rule number one.

CHERYL. Did I tell you he got my son to call me?

LORI. Rules are meant to be broken.

CHERYL. At this point, I think I can trust Stan.

LORI. Make him take you to a nice place. You're not cheap. You're in the platinum club. He needs to earn those grundies.

CHERYL. Lori, I really have to thank you.

LORI. For what?

CHERYL. You pushed me to do this. I wouldn't be here if it weren't for you.

LORI. Oh, I think you would have figured it out.

CHERYL. No, I wouldn't. I needed it. I was lost. And you... you're such a great friend and I just love you so much. Thank you for being there for me.

LORI. I love you, too. And thanks for introducing me to Dave.

CHERYL. You betcha.

(Hears a knock at the door.)

Oh, he's here.

LORI. Make him earn it.

CHERYL. See ya.

> (**LORI** *exits.* **CHERYL** *hangs up.* **CHERYL** *answers the door.* **STAN** *is there.)*

STAN. Hi, Cheryl.

CHERYL. Hi, Stan. Come on in.

STAN. *(Entering.)* Whoa! You're not a hologram. I win the bet.

CHERYL. Just my lower half. Upper half is robot.

> *(Does "the robot.")*

STAN. *(Also does "the robot.")* I *love* robots.

CHERYL. It's good to see you.

STAN. Same here. Does this mean we're friends again?

CHERYL. Well, I did invite you into my home. Which I never do.

STAN. And I thank you for your trust.

> *(Shouts to the door.)*

Bring in the chainsaw!

CHERYL. Really? A "chainsaw" joke?

STAN. I'm nervous.

CHERYL. Why?

STAN. I'm just not as comfortable in person as I am behind a computer.

CHERYL. Sometimes I feel the same way.

STAN. Hey, I'm really glad things worked out with your son.

CHERYL. Thank you so much for that. That was really big. More than you know.

STAN. No problem.

CHERYL. I didn't know you were into developing aerospace simulators.

STAN. Oh, it's something I've been working on for awhile. I just...expedited its completion.

CHERYL. Because you knew that aerospace was Justin's division at Lockheed?

STAN. Funny coincidence.

CHERYL. Uh huh. I have to ask, what did you give him to call me? A new car?

STAN. No! Absolutely not. A helicopter.

CHERYL. You better not be serious.

STAN. I didn't give him a helicopter. But they are *so* cool.

CHERYL. Then why would he talk to you? He doesn't know you.

STAN. He came up to me after the presentation. He knew my work, studied my algorithm. A fellow nerd.

CHERYL. *That* he is.

STAN. I told him what a wonderful person you are, and he bought it.

(*He laughs.*)

CHERYL. You know, sometimes maybe try...*not* being funny?

STAN. I get that a lot.

CHERYL. By the way, the renovation on the group home was unbelievably generous. Thank you so much for that.

STAN. I was happy to do it. And what better way to celebrate than by meeting in person.

CHERYL. Okay, I know I've been standoffish. It's just taken me longer than I thought to get over my husband.

STAN. I understand that, and I just wanna say, I am not looking to replace your husband.

CHERYL. And I'm not looking to replace your ex-wife.

STAN. Oh, no, that's the point. I *want* you to replace her.

CHERYL. Okay, full disclosure. I still have issues I need to deal with. Are you sure you wanna get involved in this?

STAN. "I would rather share one lifetime with you than face all the ages of this world alone."

CHERYL. That's very sweet.

STAN. That's from Arwen, *Lord of the Rings*.

CHERYL. I know. I was gonna let you have it.

STAN. So...I just want you to know, in case you were wondering, if this goes to the next level, which I hope it does... I am fully functional...

(A beat.)

...down there.

CHERYL. Wow. Not at the top of my need-to-know list, but...thank you?

STAN. Okay, that was inappropriate. Can I have a do-over?

CHERYL. Nope, the damage is done.

STAN. Dangit.

CHERYL. So...what can I get you? A Stan Jensen Napa Cabernet? I hear they're good.

STAN. Oh, gosh, how about...a hug?

CHERYL. *Whoa!* Slow down.

STAN. Sorry, sorry. You're right. The hug comes after a year, then parental permission, then the written waiver witnessed by Judge Judy, then –

(**CHERYL** *kisses then hugs* **STAN**. *Stan's phone rings.*)

(*Lights up, stage left.* **DAVE** *enters on a platform, on his cell phone with a glass of wine.* **STAN** *ignores the call.*)

DAVE. Stan usually picks up.

(**LORI** *enters on the same platform as* **DAVE**, *wearing a bathrobe, with a glass of wine.*)

LORI. They must be busy.

DAVE. Hmm. So, do you work, or...?

LORI. I'm a kindergarten teacher.

(**STAN** *and* **CHERYL** *break their embrace.*)

DAVE. Then I better behave.

LORI. No need.

(**DAVE** *and* **LORI** *smile, touch glasses and drink.*)

STAN. I guess Dave is going out with Lori tonight.

CHERYL. I heard. How do you think *that'll* end up?

STAN. Oh, it'll be a disaster.

CHERYL. Totally.

(*Music starts to play.**)

DAVE. You like music?

LORI. I love music.

(**DAVE** *and* **LORI** *put their glasses down.*)

---

* A license to produce *Love...or Best Offer* does not include a performance license for any third-party or copyrighted music. Licensees should create an original composition or use music in the public domain. For further information, please see the Music and Third-Party Materials Use Note on page iii.

STAN. Care to dance?

CHERYL. Only if you bust a move.

STAN. Oh, it's on.

> (**STAN** *and* **CHERYL** *start dancing.* **DAVE** *and* **LORI** *dance.*)

DAVE. I hope my big feet don't get in the way.

LORI. *(To the audience.) I* do.

STAN. Ready for the big finish!?

CHERYL. Bring it!

> (**STAN** *"busts a move," then pulls a groin muscle.*)

STAN. *(Groans.)* Ahh!

CHERYL. I'll get some ice!

> *(Blackout.)*

End of Play

PROPS & COSTUMES

FURNITURE

2 tables (36" × 36") stage right and left

2 chairs, one at each table

PLATFORMS

2 platforms (4'W × 4'L × 4"H) center stage right and center stage left for Lori and Dave's "on phone" entrances

PROPS

4 cell phones, (for Cheryl, Stan, Lori & Dave) Bluetooth ear pieces optional

2 laptop computers (one on each desk)

2 Lord of the Rings figurines (on Stan's desk)

2 coffee cups (for Cheryl and Stan)

3 glasses of red wine (for Cheryl, Lori and Dave)

1 Big Gulp Cup with straw (for Stan)

2 BLT sandwiches (for Cheryl and Stan – can get fake ones online)

1 cartoony Halloween mask (for Stan's mask bit)

COSTUMES

Casual clothes.

There are several short scenes with quick changes. To make the quick changes simple, rotating four or five shirts or pullover tops or blazers might help to show the passage of time when days pass between scenes. Keeping the same pants throughout the play might help with quick costume changes.

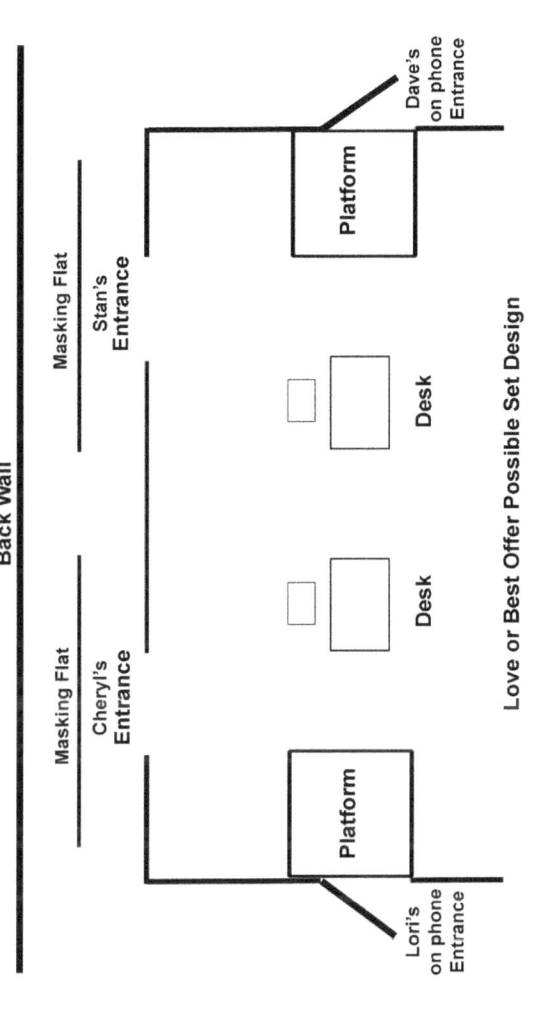

Back Wall

Masking Flat

Masking Flat

Cheryl's Entrance

Stan's Entrance

Platform

Platform

Desk

Desk

Lori's on phone Entrance

Dave's on phone Entrance

Love or Best Offer Possible Set Design